"You're in quite a hurry," Linda Jean observed.

"Well, I only have half an hour," I said. "I have to go look for my rosin and come back in time to practice."

Linda Jean looked at me strangely as she kept pace alongside. "Joy, I'm your best friend. You can tell me if you're upset. Please tell me if you're going to do something besides get rosin."

"Why would you think that?" I snapped. "I wouldn't lie to you."

"Because I saw rosin in your bag earlier," Linda Jean said softly.

That did it. My nerves snapped. "How dare you go through my things?" I yelled.

"You asked me to get your pen for you, remember? I wasn't snooping," she said.

I had to get away from Linda Jean. I had an important job to do and I wasn't going to let her stop me.

Enjoy all of The Forever Friends Club adventures. Don't miss any of the exciting books in this series:

#1   Let's Be Friends Forever!
#2   Friends to the Rescue!
#3   Keeping Secrets, Keeping Friends!
#4   That's What Friends Are For!
#5   Friends Save the Day!
#6   New Friend Blues
#7   More Than Just a Friend

# Even Best Friends Say Good-Bye

Cindy Savage

Cover illustration by Richard Kriegler

*To Terri—*
*a true friend across the miles*

Published by Willowisp Press, Inc.
401 E. Wilson Bridge Road, Worthington, Ohio 43085

Printed in the United States of America

10 9 8 7 6 5 4 3 2 1

ISBN 0-87406-446-5

# *One*

I looked around my living room at the faces of my best friends in the whole world. Linda Jean Jacobs sat on the couch stuffing her face with potato chips and flipping through the pages of her latest *Junior Scientist Magazine*. Her light brown hair had escaped from its ponytail and hung in wisps around her face.

Next to her sat Aimee Lawrence, her dark face deep in concentration. She whipped her hook in and out of the vest that she was crocheting.

Curled up in the wooden rocking chair, Kristina Branch jotted down items on our list for the party we were giving that evening. Krissy was the organized one of the group. She had her long blond curls pulled up on top of her head in a business-like bun and she had a pencil stuck over her ear.

And finally there was our new red-haired friend, Patricia Baker. Tish listened to the business of the Forever Friends Club meeting with one ear while humming to the beat on her portable headset with the other.

Yep, everything was the same as always for the Forever Friends. Except for me, Joy Marshall. I looked in the mirror over the buffet and stared back at my short, straight, brown hair. It looked lifeless and dull. My brown eyes looked scared and sad. I hoped no one could tell how worried I was, because I really wasn't ready to talk about what was bothering me.

On the surface nothing had really changed. The Forever Friends had been spending time together in my house since we were babies. We had started our business, Party Time, in this very room. My mom, Abby, was like a second mother to all of my friends.

What were my friends going to say when I told them my awful news?

"You never did tell us how your trip to Galactica went," Linda Jean said. "We were all stuck here in boring old Atlanta while you spent a crazy weekend in outer space."

I forced a laugh, even though I didn't feel

like laughing. "Outer space? Galactica is just south of Macon. It's only a theme park, after all," I told her.

"Only the best, new theme park in the world. Maybe in the universe!" Krissy corrected me. "I've been trying to talk my parents into taking our family on vacation there since we heard it was going to be built two years ago. Kitty would go crazy with all that cinematic junk going on."

Kitty is Krissy's little sister. She's a model and also does commercials. Just recently she landed a role for a movie that was being filmed in Atlanta.

But even thinking about Kitty's new movie couldn't cheer me up. The fact is, I hate change and I knew that there was a big one coming up.

I thought about when Abby decided to go back to work after my two sisters moved out. I was crushed. I thought my nice, easy life of having friends over every day was coming to an end. But things had worked out for the best. Abby had given us all jobs and we had started Party Time.

But now she and my dad were thinking about making another change—and somehow

I knew that this one wouldn't work out for the best.

"Joy's daydreaming again," Aimee said, breaking into my thoughts. "Every time we mention Galactica, she goes off into her own little world. I think something's going on."

"Did you meet someone special while you were there?" Tish asked bluntly. Tish rarely beat around the bush. She just said what she thought. She tossed her flame-colored hair over her shoulder and waited for my reply.

"No, I didn't meet anyone," I said. "And all I can think about is Russell anyway. I can't wait until his ballet company comes here from New York. Did I tell you they are going to be performing for three weeks at the Fox Theater?"

"Only about 50 times," Krissy said with a laugh. "What you didn't tell us about was Galactica. Did you go on the Solar Express ride? Was it as fabulous as they say it is?"

"Uh, yeah. The ride was great," I mumbled. But my mind was wandering again. This time I was thinking about good things—like about Russell's visit. I had met Russell when the Forever Friends went to New York to give a party for Alissa O'Toole, a famous movie star

8

who's our age. Through Alissa, I had gotten a part in the Nutcracker ballet and Russell had been my partner.

But I might miss my chance to see him again if Abby followed through on her latest plan. I liked writing to him, but after six months, I wanted to see him in person.

"She's off in Never-Never Land again," Linda Jean said, waving her hand in my direction. "Forget it. We'll try to get something out of Abby about Galactica after the party."

I knew I should be more open to my friends. After all, they didn't know why I was so upset and why I didn't really feel like talking about Galactica. And it wasn't their fault that Abby was about to ruin my life!

If only Abby wasn't so good at catering big parties. If only Pride Supermarkets hadn't had their annual convention at Galactica last week and my father hadn't been the main speaker. If only Abby hadn't met Mr. Mitchem, the owner of the park, and mentioned her business. Maybe then they wouldn't have asked Abby to cater their benefit next weekend for endangered sea mammals.

Until all that happened I had been having a great time at Galactica. It had been especially fun to spend time with my dad, since he's not home all that much. He's usually off traveling up and down the coast training new managers for Pride Supermarkets.

While I had been thinking about all the events that occurred during one brief family vacation, my friends had packed everything up for the party and were waiting for me at the door.

"Is there something wrong, Joy?" Linda Jean whispered as we carried the balloons and party favors to the station wagon.

"Yes, as a matter of fact there is," I told her, finally ready to pour all my feelings out to my best friend. But just then Abby walked up behind us.

"After the party, I'm treating everyone to ice cream at Juliet's." Abby said, interrupting. "I have an announcement to make and it concerns all of you."

"What is it, Abby? You can tell us now," Krissy insisted. Abby just smiled, but I was boiling inside—how could she smile at a time like this?

"No. After the party is soon enough," she said. "Do all of you have your stuff? Krissy, do you have your clown outfit? Joy, your dancing shoes? Linda Jean, do you have whatever ingredients you need for your science experiment? Tish, is your voice in good shape?"

Everyone nodded their heads. All of us have our own special talents that we use when we give parties. I dance, Aimee does crafts, Linda Jean does science projects, Krissy does magic tricks, and Tish does impressions.

"Let's go," Abby said.

As parties go, the one we gave that night for ten-year-old Marsha Wheeler was fantastic. The theme was Nifty Fifties. The girls were dressed in fiftes outfits—sweaters and full skirts and tennis shoes with bobby socks. I was planning to teach them some fifties dances that I had learned from a videotape.

But my heart wasn't in it. I tried to stop thinking about Abby's big announcement while the party was going on, but I just couldn't put it out of my mind. What would everyone say? I was sure they'd be as upset as I was. Aimee had just finished her craft when Linda Jean called to the group from the party table. "I need some help making the Rooti-Tutti-Frutti punch," she said. "Any volunteers?"

The girls all yelled, "YEAH!" as they scurried over to the table.

"Okay, Marsha," Linda Jean said to the birthday girl. "You put the orange juice in the punch bowl."

I watched from the sidelines as Marsha poured the cans of juice concentrate into the crystal bowl.

How many more parties would we have like this before...before...? I couldn't bear to think about it!

"Hey, Joy, would you hand us the sherbet out of the freezer?"

"Sure," I said, sniffing back my tears. I handed the containers of sherbet to Janine, a cute little girl with a big, pink bow around her ponytail.

She and Diedre, her sister, began scooping large chunks of sherbet into the punch bowl. It fizzed and melted into the punch.

Then Abby brought out the cake, a fabulous replica of an old-fashioned record player with chocolate cookies decorated as records sticking out of the top.

"This is the best birthday ever," Marsha exclaimed as she blew out her 10 candles.

All the girls clapped and cheered, then they dug into their cake.

I just couldn't take it anymore. I turned away as I felt a tear trickle out of the corner of my eye. Things were going so well. Why did they have to change?

———

———

# Two

"SO, what's this big announcement you're going to make?" Krissy asked as soon as we were all seated at our usual table at Juliet's.

Abby laughed. "Wait, give me a chance to open the menu."

*How could she think of eating at a time like this?*

"You're not thinking of starting a new business are you?" Linda Jean asked. "We're just getting used to being caterers and party planners."

"No, I plan to be a caterer for a long time," Abby told her.

*Yeah, lead them on, Abby,* I said to myself.

Abby didn't say a word about the big announcement until we ordered and were waiting for our ice cream. And I didn't say anything at all. I knew if I opened my mouth I would scream.

"All right, everyone," Abby said. "Here it is, the big news. It's a question, actually. How would you all like to go on a trip to perform at Galactica?"

After one stunned second, everyone began talking at once—except for me. I knew that there was a hitch.

"How did you manage that?" Aimee asked.

"I can't wait!" Tish exclaimed.

"I thought that they only hired older kids for parks like that. You have to be in high school to work at Six Flags," Krissy said.

"Yeah, what's really going on here?" Linda Jean asked.

"I never could fool you, Linda Jean," Abby remarked. "The rest of the story is that I have a chance to get a permanent job at Galactica. They do regular benefits to help wildlife organizations, world hunger, community projects, and other issues. Anyway, they've asked me if I'd like to be the coordinator of catering for park functions."

"Wow! That's great," Krissy said. "So you'd have to travel down there a couple of times a month to do these events?"

I couldn't stand it anymore. "No," I practically shouted. "We'd have to move!"

"MOVE!" the group all shouted at once.

"Now, it's not as bad as you may think," Abby said. "There are a lot of pluses to moving. For one thing, Mr. Marshall wouldn't have to travel anymore. The headquarters and shipping warehouses for Pride Supermarkets are in Perry, the town next to the park. If I got the job, John could transfer there permanently and do all of his training sessions from the home office.

Abby ignored our stricken expressions and continued. "Also, I wouldn't have to go out looking for new clients all the time. I'd have a steady income."

"But Abby, all of our friends are here—not to mention our family," I protested. "And all of your customers here depend on you. What about the Georgian School and the garden club?"

"I'm sure that I'll be traveling back and forth for a while until we get settled. Don't worry. I won't abandon you or my clients."

"But what about us?" Krissy asked. "Where will we go after school and during summers?"

"You all are too old for a baby-sitter anyway," Abby said. "Lots of kids your age stay by themselves after school. I'm sure all of your parents will be able to think of something."

Aimee studied the ice cream dripping down her cone. "I guess I could go to Dad's television studio every day instead of coming home. You could come, too. I'm sure my dad could use more volunteers."

"But what about the business?" Tish asked. "I was just getting used to everything."

I remained silent during the whole conversation. *Let Abby answer all the questions,* I thought. It was all her fault. She was the one wrecking all of our lives. I decided that I wasn't going to be sad anymore. I'd be mad. It was easier to be mad at Abby than to face the future.

Suddenly, Linda Jean looked at me, tears teetering on the edge of her eyelashes. "Hey, we're all worried about places to go and running the business, but the worst part is that we'll be losing Joy and Abby. They're the reason we have a club in the first place."

Abby looked at each one of us in turn. Her eyes shimmered with tears, but I turned away, determined not to let her get to me.

"I know that this has come as a big shock to all of you, but change isn't so bad. In fact, lots of good things could come out of this move," she said.

"Like what?" Aimee asked.

"Like becoming more independent young women and learning how to rely on your own instincts. And meeting new friends," she added, looking directly at me.

"And we'll still see each other," Abby continued. "Galactica is only two and a half hours away, not a million miles. And think how much fun it will be to have year-round passes to the park. And we'll be right near the river and within 30 minutes of the lake. We can go sailing, waterskiing, canoeing..."

"And we'll get sand in all of our clothes, smell like rotting fish all the time..."

"That's enough, Joy. I know you're not thrilled, but in time you'll see what a good move it could be for the family."

"It sounds as if it's all settled," Tish said, looking worried.

"Well, not exactly. This job that I'm inviting you on is my tryout. The park is giving a benefit for Coastline Conservations and they expect to have as many children as adults attend. I told them about Party Time and they agreed to hire you as well. You'll all get free passes to the rides and they'll put us up in the Stardust Hotel. Isn't it exciting?"

"Sounds more like something out of a bad movie," I muttered.

"I wish you could try to find something positive in this adventure," Abby told me. "Nothing is certain yet, but even if I do get the job and we have to move, we should try to have fun and enjoy the trip."

Everyone but me smiled reluctantly.

"Well, going to Galactica will probably be fun," Tish admitted.

"It's probably the best job we'll ever have," Krissy added.

"You know, I heard that they have one ride that makes you feel just like an astronaut. They spin you around in one of those centrifuge things until you feel the G-force," Linda Jean said. "My friend Nick told me about it at the skating rink last week."

As I sat back and listened to the conversation around me, I wondered if my friends had forgotten the real issue because they were so excited about seeing Georgia's newest tourist attraction. They no longer appeared even the least little bit upset that we might leave Atlanta and maybe never see them again. Now I knew how Tish felt when her parents moved her all over the world to different military posts.

I had to do something about this—and fast—before the Forever Friends Club fell apart.

The next day was Sunday. I strolled over to Linda Jean's house right after breakfast. I didn't bother knocking on the front door. I knew she would be out back feeding her animals. Even though she had given most of them to Orchid Gardens Retirement Center for the Pets for Seniors program, she still had a mini zoo.

"Are you back here, Linda Jean?" I called as I came around the house.

"I'm on the patio," she called back. "Down, Mascot," I heard from around back. "I know you're hungry, but my arm isn't your breakfast."

"Pretty strange diet you feed your pets," I teased, coming around the corner.

"I think he's teething," she explained. "He's still a baby you know."

"I don't think of 100 pound dogs as babies," I chuckled.

"He may look grown up, but he still acts like a puppy." To prove her point she threw a hunk of wood out into the yard. Mascot bounded after it and caught it in midair. He was back putting it in her hand in no time.

She laughed. "Now look what I've started. Joy, will you please give Mac his seed?" She threw the stick again.

I poured birdseed and vegetables into the macaw's dish and wondered how I was going to open up the subject of moving. I knew if anyone would help me figure out a way to stop the move it was Linda Jean. She had been closest to me since she moved here three years ago from California. I had helped her out when she wanted to talk about her new stepfamily.

Luckily she seemed to sense that I was having trouble saying what was on my mind. "I noticed that you aren't too happy about this move," Linda Jean said bluntly.

"You noticed, huh?"

"It was hard to miss."

"I thought I hid it better than that. Everyone seemed so excited. Nobody cares that I might be moving."

"That's not true," Linda Jean put down the

stick and came over to me. "None of us want you to move. Is that what you think?"

"It sure seemed like it last night."

"You have to admit that most kids would love to have their parents work in a place like that. It's like living a fantasy life."

"But I don't want to leave here. I love my house. I love my school. I love my pool. But most of all I love my friends. What will I do without you?"

We sat next to each other on a wooden bench in Linda Jean's backyard. "It certainly will be different around here without you," Linda Jean agreed.

"It would be a disaster," I moaned. "And I'm not going to just sit still and let it happen."

Linda Jean looked up. "What are you going to do about it? You know your mom won't fail the tryout."

"Maybe not on her own. But maybe we could do something to ruin it for her. Nothing to hurt her reputation of course. But maybe enough to make them think twice about the job offer."

"I don't know," Linda Jean said. "It sounds risky. And not very nice. How could you do that to your mom?"

I shook my head. Then I brought my knees up and rested my chin on them. "I'm desperate," I told her. "Who knows?" Maybe if I keep bringing up all the bad points about the move, it will discourage her."

"Like what?" Linda Jean asked.

"Like overcrowded schools, crime rates, and pollution."

"We have those problems in Atlanta," Linda Jean reminded me.

"Would you consider hiding me in your spare bedroom if I ran away?" I asked her.

"Running away wouldn't do any good. I thought about running away when I was going to have to go visit my mom and her new stepfamily last summer. I just about went crazy trying to think of reasons not to go."

"But that turned out great. Your mom ended up moving to Atlanta and Stephanie and Josh turned out to be okay kids."

Linda Jean toyed with Mascot's leash, twirling it over and over between her fingers. "But I was really afraid that Mom getting married to Lewis would change everything. I was scared I'd have to move back in with her, or that she would forget about me once she had two new kids. But most of all, do you know what I was scared of?"

"No, what?" I asked.

"I was scared that I might like her new family and then I wouldn't have a good reason to be mad anymore."

"Well, I'll never stop being mad about this," I insisted. "This move will ruin too many of my plans. I mean, besides not being with my friends, look at all the other stuff I'll be missing. I'll miss performing in the summer recital with the ballet workshop and Russell's visit next weekend."

"He'll be here for three weeks," Linda Jean said.

"But I wanted to see him that first day. I had planned to visit him before his first performance."

"Abby would say you're being unreasonable," Linda Jean warned.

I knew Linda Jean was just trying to help me see all sides, but I didn't want to feel guilty about my anger. I squared my shoulders and tipped up my chin. "Abby hasn't even seen how unreasonable I can be!"

# Three

"IS everybody ready?" Abby asked for the third time.

"Not yet," I replied. "I think I have to go to the bathroom again."

Abby sighed. "Well, get on with it. I'd like to be there on time so that I can make a good impression."

*That's what I want to make,* I thought to myself, *an impression.*

The Forever Friends were all loaded into the station wagon with my mother and father, and enough supplies to do parties for a whole month in Galactica. We were on our way there for Abby's tryout and our performance.

I should have been excited. I should have been grateful for the opportunity. I should have at least been proud of Abby for being

27

good enough to be offered this job.

But I wasn't. All I could think about was sabotage. All I had thought about for the past four days had been sabotage—either sabotage or running away.

I had even called Liza to ask if I could move in with her and be Jeremiah's nanny. "I'll be perfect," I had told her. "And I'll clean your house, too."

Liza had been sympathetic, but firm. "We'd love to have you, but we don't have room," she had said. "Besides, we've been looking for an excuse to move out of Atlanta and now we have it. Maybe the whole family will end up in Galactica."

"But not my friends," I wailed.

"Try to think about Mom and Dad," Liza had said. "Think how long Dad's job has kept them apart and what it would mean to them to be together again."

I tried to think about that. I really did. But all I could think about was how Mom and Dad being together would mean that I would be apart from my Forever Friends.

As I strolled slowly out to the car, I thought about it some more. I had no choice. I had to stick to my plan of sabotage.

"Did you remember to lock the front door?" Abby asked as I got into the car.

"Oops," I said, snapping my fingers. "I guess I forgot." I strolled slowly back to the house and locked the door.

Then I sauntered back to the car.

"I'm not feeling very well, Abby," I said, clutching my stomach. "I think I may get carsick."

"Nonsense," John said. "You've never been carsick in your life."

"There's always a first time. And it's so hot," I said, wiping imaginary drops of sweat off of my forehead. "We're all going to roast. Why don't we wait and leave in the evening?"

"Because we want to see some of the sights before we have to go to work," Abby said. "And besides, the car has air-conditioning."

I sighed and got into the car. I didn't think I could delay the trip any longer.

Tish, Aimee, and Krissy were all chattering in the back seats. But Linda Jean was watching me. She knew what I was up to. I had a plan—a plan to convince Abby that making the move to Galactica was a bad idea.

I had never been very good at whining, but I was learning fast. The traffic was terrible. I had stalled long enough that we were going to be stuck in rush-hour traffic for sure!

"All right, let me explain the schedule," Abby said as soon as we were on the highway. "We'll work tonight after dinner. Then Saturday, tomorrow, we'll do the bulk of the food preparation. But you'll still have time to practice your routines in the afternoon on the stage. And you'll have time to check out the rides."

"I can't wait!" Tish said.

"After dinner on Saturday we'll make the cinnamon buns so that they'll be fresh for the breakfast meeting on Sunday morning. We'll be serving breakfast, lunch, and dinner on Sunday and your performance will be during dinner—" Abby continued.

"Oh, no!" I exclaimed suddenly, cutting her off. "I forgot my ballet slippers. I can't perform at the party without my toe shoes."

John sighed and looked at Abby.

I kept my face straight. I didn't want them to know that I left them home on purpose.

"I guess we'll have to go back for them," John said. He took the next exit and crawled the car back through Friday morning rush-hour traffic to Honeybee Court.

I ran in and retrieved my slippers from the back of the closet. Then I ran back to the car.

"Anyone else leave anything behind?" John asked as I buckled my seatbelt once again.

There was a chorus of *no* from the back.

"I'm really thirsty, though," I mentioned as we started rolling again. "Why don't we stop on the way out and pick up some juice?"

"Great idea," Abby surprised me. "We may as well wait for the traffic to break up a little anyway. John, let's go to the drive through at Sparky's."

So Dad drove the long way around Atlanta to avoid traffic and to buy us all juice at Sparky's. I asked if we could go in, but Abby firmly insisted on the drive-through window.

"Thanks, Abby, John," Krissy said, after taking a swig of her juice. "This orange juice is a real pick me up. I'm afraid I didn't get much sleep last night."

"Oh, why is that?" I asked. Krissy looked perky enough to me. She even had a red ribbon in her hair that matched her red tank top. "Did you have an upset stomach?"

"No. I was thinking about the trip, I guess. Remember New York?" she asked the others. "We had so much fun there, going shopping and skating and watching Joy perform with the New York City Ballet."

"You did that?" Tish asked me. "Wow! I'm impressed."

I kept forgetting that Tish hadn't been a member of the Forever Friends Club back then. She had moved to Atlanta just a few months ago, but it seemed as if we had known her all of her life. I felt the same way about Linda Jean.

Oh, it's not that we never have problems, but we seem to be able to work them out together. I wasn't sure that we would be able to do that long distance.

Thinking of that made me even more determined to delay and ruin this trip. I hated to be this way to my parents, because usually they were the best parents a girl could hope for. But this time they were making a mistake. I knew they would thank me for my trouble later.

I joined back into the conversation about New York. As it happened we were just driving by the Fox Theater at that moment.

"I really wish I had been able to see Russell on his first day here," I said with a sigh. "He'll be in a strange, new city and will need a friend.

Maybe we should just drop in for a minute."

Abby looked at me as if I were a creature from another planet. "What's with you today, Joy?" she asked. "You know we're on a schedule. Besides, Russell isn't due to arrive until this afternoon sometime. And he'll want to rest after his flight. There will be plenty of time to see him when we get back."

"But then you'll want me to pack, and you'll want to get the house ready to sell, and there won't be time."

"Honey, relax," John said, putting his arm around my shoulders. "Your young man will still be there and I promise you'll see him. I want to see this dynamo dancer myself. From what you tell me, he sounds as if he's the next Mikhail Baryshnikov."

I giggled in spite of myself. "Well, maybe not that good. But he's already determined to make dancing his career, just like I am."

I can see it all now," Aimee teased. "Russell and Joy will have their names up in lights. Crowds of people dressed in tuxedos and evening gowns will be pushing and shoving their way into the theater to see the performance. Flash bulbs will be popping, TV cameras will be rolling..."

"Oh, quit it," I said. But I had to admit that I had imagined the same thing myself.

As we drove down highway 75 out of Atlanta and passed the exit sign for McDonough, I casually mentioned the next problem.

"Oh, no!" I exclaimed, using the same tone of voice I had used before.

"What now?" Abby asked.

"I think I left the water running in the bathroom sink."

"And why do you think you did that?" she asked.

"Well, I was washing my face and I put the plug in so I could splash cold water on after the hot. You know how they tell you to do so that your pores close?"

Abby nodded, keeping her eyes straight ahead.

"Well, then I had to rush so much to leave, that I think I may have left it running. Just a dribble," I added. "But I suppose that the washrag I left in there could clog up the drain and it could flood."

Abby's look clearly said that she was onto me.

*Innocent*, I thought to myself. *Act innocent.*

"Well I guess we'll have to turn around and go back," I said.

"We'll do no such thing," Abby said. "We'll pull over on the next exit and call the Lawrences. They have a key."

"I don't think they're home," Aimee said. I could have hugged her for saying that!

"Well then, we'll call all the neighbors or Liza or Mary until we find one person who can solve the problem. We are *not*, and I repeat, *not* driving an hour back up the road even if we flood the whole house!"

Linda Jean widened her eyes and she shook her head a little. I decided not to press my luck any farther.

"I'm sorry. It was an accident," I told them after John had succeeded in contacting Mr. Jacobs, Linda Jean's dad, and had him check on the water.

"Of course it was an accident," John said. "We know you wouldn't do something like that on purpose."

*Or would I?*

# *Four*

BEFORE we knew it, we were there. My stalling hadn't done any good at all!

"Look at the streets," Aimee said, pointing out her window. "They look like they're real silver!"

"And check out the street lights. They look like tiny flying saucers," Linda Jean added.

"The shops are amazing. I've never seen so much neon," Tish said.

Everything was shiny and modern—from the robotic garbage cans on the streets to the mirrored windows of our hotel.

"I feel as if we just went through a time machine and landed 1,000 years into the future," Krissy said. "But it doesn't look too unnatural. There are lots of plants and even a beautiful fountain over there."

"Do people actually live here?" I asked, trying to sound bored. "Or do they just come to visit?"

"Mr. Mitchem told me that 2,000 people live here and work at the park. It has always been his dream to build a town from the ground up. Prospective residents have to agree to conform to certain building requirements if they want to build a house. The whole town will have the same architecture.

"Doesn't that seem a little boring?" I asked, staring out the window and putting on my bored expression.

"Only if you like antiques, I guess," John joked. "I kind of like it."

"I like Atlanta," I mumbled.

Everyone ignored me, and we went into the hotel.

As we walked inside, I couldn't help thinking that no matter what Linda Jean said, I didn't think the others were nearly as upset about this move as I was. Or were they just so distracted by the glitz of Galactica that they had forgotten the real reason why we all were here?

"We'll take this stuff up to the rooms. Then Abby and I have to meet with the real estate agent," John said. "Would you like to go, Joy?"

"No, thanks. It doesn't matter what I think. You'll buy whatever house you want anyway," I said.

"Why don't you girls go over to the park and have a look around?" Abby suggested. I guess she was pretending that she hadn't heard the sarcastic tone of my voice. "We'll meet you for dinner at the Meteor Cafe. You can't miss it. It's right underneath the Star Gazer Telescope and Observatory."

"Boy, Abby, you really know your way around," Krissy remarked.

"Well, John and I love this place. We really checked it out last time we were here. And I'm sure Joy will like living here once she gets used to the idea."

"You haven't gotten the job yet," I said softly.

"I don't know why you're giving Abby such a hard time about this," Krissy said later as we strolled through the gates of the park onto Asteroid Avenue. "This is a fantastic place! I'd like to move here, too."

"Fine, then you take my place, Krissy, and I'll stay at your house. I get along just fine with your sister. Maybe nobody would mind if we switched lives," I suggested.

"Right," Krissy said laughing. I guess she thought I was joking or something.

"Here it is," Linda Jean said. "The Solar Express. This is the ride I've been dying to go on. Come on, Joy. Let's have some fun while we're here, okay?"

Before I could answer, Linda Jean pulled me toward the entrance of the Solar Express. "You're going to love this," she assured me.

"I've already been on it, remember?"

"Then I'm going to love it!" she said excitedly. We followed the rest of the crowd into a dark tunnel. Above us tiny, blinking, colored lights mapped out the solar system and lit our journey.

There was a loud clang as a set of double doors opened and closed in front of us. The door seemed to gobble up batch after batch of tourists. A pretty attendant in a gold space suit costume beckoned to us to enter.

"Did you see her hair?" Tish whispered as we packed into the small room. "She had lights in it."

"It was just a battery pack," I informed her. "It's no big deal."

"Did anyone ever tell you that you're boring, Joy?" Aimee asked.

"Can I help it if I've seen all this before?" I snapped as the giant elevator dropped us at a fast pace into the center of the make-believe earth.

"Well excuse us for being excited. We weren't here last weekend, so this is pretty neat to all of us," Krissy said. "If you didn't want to come with us today, you could have stayed in the hotel room, you know. You didn't have to make yourself so miserable."

Were these really my Forever Friends? They had never talked to me this way. Maybe it just proved what I had been thinking since Abby announced the move. My friends didn't care if I left Atlanta or not. In fact, from the looks on their faces as we walked through layer after layer of earth to the center of the fake active volcano, any one of them would gladly take my place. *So, let them if they wanted to,* I thought.

"Stay to the center of the platform," a voice called out over the loudspeaker. "Do not touch the walls!"

Suddenly, the walls around us dropped away from the elevator and left all of us standing in a chamber designed to look like the molten lava pit of a volcano.

I could see beads of sweat appearing on people's foreheads even though the room wasn't hot. But seeing all the flames and bubbling lava made you think it really was hot. That was called the power of suggestion, which was what the park was all about.

They even had signs posted that if you had a heart condition you shouldn't go on some of the rides or through some of the exhibits. Even though I was in a bad mood, I still thought it was amazing that just thinking you were in danger could make your body react as if it really was in danger.

We walked along a smoldering cement suspension bridge that looked like wood. A blinking light in front of us pointed the way to the inner chamber.

"Wow! This is really neat," Linda Jean said when our group had reached the chamber. All around us were high-tech gadgets—computers, sensors, spaceship launchers, and communications equipment. And there were lots of robots.

"Please walk this way," said the first robot. "Pick a row and walk to the very end. Sit down and buckle your restraining device."

"Hold on to your arm grips," said another robot. We have an apprentice pilot today and sometimes it is a rough trip out of the crater."

"Is there anyone here who wants to exit the flight?" asked a third robot. "Please exit out the double doors to the left of the shuttle."

One lady got up and made her way to the exit with a small child who was crying.

"It's okay," I said to the little girl as she passed me. "We're not really flying up into outer space." She gave me an unsure smile through her tears, but insisted on leaving anyway.

I enjoyed the darkness of the room. I closed my eyes for a minute and tried to relax. I decided that I may as well stop all of my complaining for the time being. It was better if I saved my performances for Abby and John.

A funny little robot wandered out onto the stage in front of us. "Are all passengers accounted for?" he asked the audience.

"Are there any passengers on this shuttle?" he shouted "Please answer."

We all responded, "Yes!"

"Loud bunch, aren't you?" the robot asked.

The audience laughed. No one could really tell whether the robot was simply mechanized or if someone was running it. Another robot came on the stage and ran the first robot through a series of checklist-type questions, none of which he knew the answers to.

"Are hangar bay doors secured?"

"Uh,what doors?"

"Impulse power up?"

"I never can remember where that switch is," the confused robot answered.

By the time the robot got the shuttle's engine started, the audience was laughing like crazy. Then our imaginary trip began. We were supposed to be inside a volcanic shuttle launch station (the heat from the volcano powered the rocket boosters). The space school dropout robot was planning to take us on a tour of the outer galaxy—if he could get us out of the volcano!

We all watched the images on the screen in front of us. It felt like we were moving. The screens in front of us showed where we were going. The ones behind us showed where we had been. It was neat.

"This robot's crazy," Linda Jean exclaimed as he ran the ship into a garbage dumpster, narrowly missed the main computer, and swirled us around in a complete circle.

We felt every bump. We all held onto the chair arms and felt as if we were being dropped off a cliff, flung into space, spun through a time tunnel, and caught in a shower of meteors.

As we stumbled out of the chamber at the end of the ride, even I had a smile on my face. "It's hard to believe that the chamber actually only moves a few inches each way," I remarked.

"Really?" Krissy asked. "I was sure we had really spun around. I even feel dizzy."

"It's the power of suggestion," I told her. "I asked one of the employees about it last weekend. The only thing that moves is the floor. And they have air in the seats to make you think you're sinking."

"I want to go again," Linda Jean said. "This time I'm going to close my eyes and see if I can feel the movement without looking at the screens."

"You're on. Let's go," Aimee said.

As I watched the others follow Linda Jean to the entrance of the ride again, I made a decision. Stopping my parents from moving us to Galactica didn't have to be all dull. I could have fun while I was here, couldn't I?

"Hey guys, wait up!" I called.

# Five

AFTER a few hours of rides and shows, we plopped down at the Saturn Burger for a soft drink. I had tried my best to be pleasant for the remainder of the afternoon. I noticed that my friends had their heads together whispering every once in a while, but I tried not to feel left out. They were probably just talking about how stupid I was to want to stay in Atlanta when I could live practically in an amusement park.

"It's hot and I'm tired," Krissy mentioned while running the icy outside of her cup over her forehead. "Remember that heat wave right when school got out last year? I think this is worse."

I was about to mention the heat as another reason why I didn't want to move when Aimee gave Krissy a shove that I don't think I was supposed to notice.

"Oh, right," Krissy said. "I don't know what I'm complaining about. I'm having a fabulous time. When did Abby want us back to help this evening?"

"She wants us back by dinnertime," Aimee reminded us. "But I'm starving now and it's only 3:00. An ice cream cone would really hit the spot. What do you say, Joy?"

When I didn't answer, Tish jumped into the silence.

"I'm hungry, too," agreed Tish. "I wonder what they call their ice cream here—flying saucer cones?"

"Close," Linda Jean said, pointing to the menu over the shiny, silver counter. "Milky Way sundaes. Sprinkle your own stardust," she read.

"Oh come on, let's get one!" Krissy said, heading toward the ice cream shop. "After five times on the Comet Coaster, I could eat a planet, not just a sundae."

We placed our order and waited while the waiter in a space suit covered with glitter paint went to the counter to fill it. He spoke into an intercom and the order was lifted over the counter on a tray that seemed to float through the air until he took it.

"Wow," Krissy said again. "I don't know why you're so upset about having to live here. Everything is so neat. I've never seen so many cool gadgets in my life!"

"Yeah, did you see those bathrooms?" Tish asked. "The doors opened and closed automatically when you walked by."

"While I was washing my hands the towel dispenser refilled itself. Can you believe that?" Aimee asked. "The whole place seems to run by itself."

"No, it doesn't," I told her smugly. "Most of the stuff is run by computers, or by people sitting behind one-way mirrors who are working the controls. It's all fake."

"How do you know that?" Linda Jean demanded. "Did you go on a backstage tour or something?"

"Yeah, when I was here last time. We learned how everything worked. It's not nearly as magical as it looks."

"Finding out how it works makes it even more interesting to me," Linda Jean commented. "Do you think we could go on a backstage tour? I wonder if I could make robots at any of our parties. I saw robot plans in one of my junior science magazines. Hmmm...if I could just get a few more pointers."

The waiter delivered the ice cream just as I was about ready to scream or burst into tears. My friends thought Galactica was the neatest place in the world. There was no way that I would get them to help me sabotage the move plan.

The waiter set down a huge tray with bowls of ice cream, pitchers of syrups, and shakers of toppings.

"This is great," Krissy said, picking up the first bottle. She shook little, colored stars all over her ice cream. Then she spooned silver balls on and topped the whole thing off with butterscotch syrup.

There were so many toppings to choose from. Everyone was trying everything. The bottles were moving around so quickly that I just had to reach out and grab the first one I saw free. I didn't care what it tasted like anyway. Even the real Milky Way sprinkled on my ice cream wouldn't have made me feel any better.

I shook red-colored sugar over my vanilla ice cream and picked up my spoon. "We'd better get going," I said. "Abby wants us to start work right after dinner."

And I still hadn't figured out a way to ruin her tryout. I took a bite of ice cream and held it in my mouth while I tried to come up with a plan.

Suddenly my eyes started watering. My mouth felt like it was on fire. I spit out the ice cream and grabbed my ice water and drank the whole glass, then I grabbed Linda Jean's.

"What's wrong?" Aimee asked urgently.

"HOT!" I choked out, my throat raw from the little I'd swallowed.

Aimee looked down at the jar of toppings and lifted the one I had sprinkled on my sundae.

"Cayenne pepper," she read. She held it up next to the red sugar. They looked almost the same. "Are you all right?"

"More water," I croaked.

By this time the waiter had rushed back with a pitcher of ice water and a new bowl of ice cream for me.

"I keep telling the management that they need to take the burger spices off the tray when people order ice cream," he said. "Maybe they'll listen to me now. You're my second customer to do that this week. I'm really sorry."

"I'll be okay," I managed to say through my tears. "Do you have any tissues?"

"Sure. I'll be right back."

"That's awful, Joy," Tish said. "Maybe you should sue the restaurant."

"They already gave me new ice cream," I said. "I'll be fine in a minute."

"I don't know. You don't look so good," Aimee said. "Your whole face is red."

"Thanks," I told her sarcastically.

"What are friends for?" she asked.

When Tish said that I had a sudden flash of imagination. What if I substituted cayenne pepper for one of the spices in Abby's cookies? Better yet, I could mix it with the cinnamon on the cinnamon buns. The guests at the banquet would have fits and Abby would lose any chance of the job.

What a perfect plan! I smiled through my tears.

And I could get my friends to help me without them ever knowing it.

"Are you okay?" Linda Jean asked as we walked a little behind the rest of the group on our way back to the hotel.

"Not really. But I guess it doesn't matter

what I'm feeling," I told her.

Linda Jean kicked at a silver cobblestone with her toe. "I wish you didn't have to move, Joy. I hated it when I had to leave my friends in California. But then I met the Forever Friends, and you all made my new life much easier. Maybe you'll find new friends, and it will be the same for you."

"No one could replace the Forever Friends," I said with a sigh.

"And we all feel the same way about you," she assured me.

"It doesn't seem that way," I said, nodding in the direction of the laughing group in front of us.

"Everyone deals with stuff differently. Maybe Aimee, Krissy, and Tish are dealing with it by trying to pretend it isn't happening."

"But it is happening," I cried. "And faster than anyone thinks. I mean, my parents are talking about buying a house here—that's serious! This could be practically the last time we're all together."

Linda Jean's concerned look deepened into a frown. "I know," she said. "It's all happening too fast."

"Well, I'm doing everything I can to slow it down," I told her. "And after today, I think I have a foolproof plan."

The look on her face was a mixture of alarm and curiosity. "Oh, Joy, you're not really going to do anything to mess things up, are you?"

"You'll see," I hinted.

"You can tell me," she said.

"No, I can't," I replied, touching her arm lightly. "If I somehow get into trouble, I don't want anyone else involved."

# Six

THE cayenne pepper idea was good. But it wouldn't hurt to come up with a few back-up plans. After dinner, while everyone else was still washing up in our rooms, I decided to go down and help Abby.

I went on ahead to the huge stainless steel kitchen in the center of the park where all the food was prepared for the banquets.

Abby wasn't there yet, so I quickly scanned the room looking for something to delay the cooking.

Out of the corner of my eye I saw the knife rack. I hid it carefully in the storage room. Then I took the tomatoes and hid them in a lower cupboard. I put the flour in the oven and the cookie sheets way in the back, behind about 17 pots and pans.

"There," I said, brushing off my hands. "That should put us behind schedule." I hurried back to the hotel and met the others in the lobby just as they were getting ready to leave for the kitchen.

"We were wondering where you were," Linda Jean said, with a suspicious look in her eye. I wasn't fooling her. But I thanked her silently for not saying anything.

"I just came down early and then went shopping in the gift shop," I lied.

"Anything cute in there?" Aimee asked.

I glanced back at the window of the shop. "I saw some cute stained-glass ornaments and...uh, crystals," I said.

"I'll have to go in there later to check it out," she replied. "You never know when I might find another great project idea. I've been taking notes all afternoon on things to make when I get home."

Whew! They hadn't guessed that I'd been up to something. All this lying and sneaking around was very nerve-racking. What if I told them I needed their help? Would they help me ruin Abby's chances for the job?

"Isn't this terrific?" Tish asked cheerfully as we passed the decorated window of the shop. "You could spend a lifetime checking out the little nooks and crannies of this place."

Yeah, a lifetime, I thought to myself. I could spend a lifetime with a bunch of robots for friends.

Abby was all business when we reached the kitchen. She had a big pot of water heating up on the huge industrial stove. "The management representative will be here soon to watch us in action, so I'd like to get as much done as possible before she comes," Abby told us.

"What do we do first?" Krissy asked.

"First, we put on our hair nets and aprons," Tish teased. "I've only been with this outfit for a couple of months, and even I know that."

"I've made each of you a list," Abby said, passing out pieces of paper as we finished donning our nets and aprons and washing our hands again.

"Joy, you collect the ingredients for the ravioli filling. Aimee, here's a list of stuff for the dough. Linda Jean, you prepare the cutting board and all the tools for putting these little pillows together. And Tish, you get the spices."

We all rushed to the labeled cupboards and

refrigerators for our ingredients. Only I knew that we wouldn't find them where they were supposed to be. I shoved down my guilty feelings as the first cry for help came in.

"I can't find the knives," Linda Jean said, flashing a glance at me.

"There's a large block on the counter," Abby called from where she was working at the center island.

"The block's not here," Linda Jean said.

"Well, look around. It has to be somewhere."

"Where are the tomatoes?" I asked. "Has anyone seen the tomatoes?"

"In the refrigerator?" Abby asked.

"No such luck," I said, managing to achieve just the right note of surprise in my voice.

"I can't find the flour!" Aimee said.

"Where are those knives?" Linda Jean repeated.

Everyone began opening and slamming doors. The noise was irritating. Abby looked up from her recipe books to see us all frantically searching for the items on our lists.

"There isn't a cookie sheet in sight!"

"I brought those baking sheets from home especially for the cinnamon buns," Abby exclaimed. "Who could have taken them?" She finally got off her chair and came down to help us.

She went down on her knees in front of the pan cupboard and had crawled in up to her waist when we all heard a loud "Ahem!"

Abby banged her head on the counter as she came out, dislodging her bun and hair net.

"Ah, Ms. Mitchem. How good to see you again!" Abby said.

"Is there a problem, Mrs. Marshall?"

"Not at all," Abby said, smoothly tucking a stray hair back into her bun and rearranging her hair net. "And how is your father, and all of the other members of the board?"

Ms. Mitchem looked around the spotless kitchen. "In spite of the fact that my father owns this park, how he is doing has nothing to do with why I'm here."

"Why are you here?" Abby asked, the hint of a smile on the corners of her lips.

I held my breath. Maybe Ms. Mitchem would fire Abby right there on the spot!

"I thought you would be working by this time," Ms. Mitchem snapped. "I don't see anything being made."

"Well, you know, catering is a complicated

business, Ms. Mitchem," Abby said, her smile growing. "Getting set up to begin is just as important as the actual preparation of the food."

"I must remind you that I was not in favor of selecting you for this job," Ms. Mitchem said mightily. "The board of directors out-voted me in what I can only assume was a fit of goodwill during last week's convention. It is highly irregular to offer someone a tryout without extensive investigation into her background."

Abby stood up straight and put on a no-nonsense face. "I have delivered my qualifications and references to the board and I would appreciate it if you would talk to the board before making accusations."

"My, my, aren't we touchy?" Ms. Mitchem remarked. "I'm certainly not making accusations. I'm only stating the facts. You can be sure I will be monitoring your progress at frequent intervals. And I will write down any and all problems or deviations from the schedule that I see."

She looked at the large, white kitchen clock on the wall. "Six o'clock," she murmured and jotted down something on her clipboard. She read aloud, "Mrs. Marshall found crawling into the pan cupboard."

"Oh, Abby," Aimee exclaimed when Ms. Mitchem had finally left. "She's awful. I thought you said the people were all nice down here."

"Most of them are. The ones that offered me the job were very supportive. Apparently Ms. Mitchem wants her sister to get the job and was pressuring the board to choose her for the job before the members tried out any other caterers. I'm sure she'll come around."

"I doubt it," I said gloomily. "Even if you get the job, she'll probably make your life miserable until you quit."

"I've never been one to run away from a challenge," Abby declared. "I know she doesn't like me, but she's not the only member on the board. As long as my star employees don't give up on me, I can do anything!"

"Gosh, Abby," Linda Jean giggled. "You're even beginning to sound like this place—star employees—get it?"

"Well let's power up and find the rest of our ingredients," Krissy joked.

"Yes," agreed Tish. "We'll scan the area for what's missing! Beep...beep...beep." She imitated a radar screen.

Krissy pulled the bag of tomatoes out of the lower cupboard at the same time Abby unearthed the cookie sheets from the back of the pan storage area.

"Do you think Ms. Mitchem could have hidden these things just to get you flustered?" Krissy asked.

Abby shook her head. "I don't think so. Ms. Mitchem doesn't like me, that's for sure. But I don't think she would stoop to hiding ingredients to make us late on purpose. That's pretty low."

I cringed when Abby said that. But I knew that I had to keep to my plan. I could barely stand to look at Abby as she discussed the possible reasons that the supplies had been misplaced.

At that moment, the double doors into the kitchen area burst open again and John entered. I knew that he could tell that something was wrong by the frown on his face.

"What's up?" he asked.

"Could be my job if we don't get busy on this stuff. But I'm going to have to go buy some extra spices. They seem to be missing."

"I thought you brought everything you needed," John said.

"I thought I did, too. And I took inventory when we arrived, but when we met here tonight, nothing was where I left it. And, to make matters worse, Ms. Mitchem showed up."

"Oh, her," John said with a sigh. "Don't let her get to you."

"It's hard not to. She seems like she's really out to get me," Abby said. "Maybe I should forget the whole thing."

*That's the spirit, Abby,* I thought.

I decided I'd better say something sympathetic or else people would begin to suspect that the whole thing was my fault.

"You can do it, Abby," I said quietly, hoping my voice would just blend in with the rest.

But Abby was quick to pick up on my encouragement. "Do you really think so?" she asked, looking at me with a serious expression.

I had to turn away. "Yes, I do. Remember what you always say, *'Can't* never did anything.'"

"You're so right. Let's have one more search around this kitchen and see if we can find those spices. Then we'll whip up the biggest, best batch of ravioli that the universe has ever seen."

I groaned. Now she was more determined than ever, and I was the cause of that, too!

My father found the spices. "Maybe we should dust for fingerprints," he said.

I froze. Was I going to be found out?

Then Abby started laughing, her frustration melting away. "We could post an all-night guard."

"How about one of those robots?" Linda Jean suggested. "With a hidden camera."

*A big help you are, LJ,* I thought.

"So what about dessert?" Dad asked after we had all pitched in and cooked up a huge batch of homemade ravioli and a big pot of sauce.

"You go on and take the girls, John," Abby said. "I'm going to clean up here and take inventory again. I want to make sure there isn't a repeat of tonight when we have to do most of the preparations tomorrow."

We all followed John outside. But I didn't want to be with the laughing, chattering group congratulating themselves on overcoming the missing ingredient mix-up. Instead, I wanted to be alone—to think.

"Do you mind if I beg off of dessert tonight, John?" I asked him as we were walking back toward the hotel to change. "I think I ate too much this afternoon and I'd like to just take a walk," I added.

He studied my face, but I kept it blank.

"Are you sure you'll be all right?" he asked.

"I'll stay in the park and be home before they turn off the lights. Okay?"

Dad kissed me on the top of the head. "I know this is tough on you, sweetie. If you need anything, Abby should be back at the hotel in an hour or so."

"Thanks," I mumbled.

# *Seven*

I wandered off toward the bright lights of Asteroid Avenue. *This is what it would be like if we moved here,* I thought. There would be people and activity all around, but I would be alone.

The Forever Friends would be off doing something together and pretty soon I would be just someone that they write to like Alissa and Russell in New York.

I thought about Russell. What was he doing now? Practicing at the Fox Theater? The Fox Theater was putting on a special program called Christmas in July and the New York City Ballet was performing its specialty, *The Nutcracker.*

How I wished I was there under those lights instead of in the glaring, artificial world of

Galactica. I remembered dancing with Russell as if it were yesterday. His jumps were so smooth and his lifts seemed effortless. I could almost smell the rosin on my shoes and taste the anticipation before the curtain went up.

Then I realized that I really was smelling rosin and I could hear the roar of a crowd. I looked up from the path to see the lighted marquee of the Orbit Palace. I followed the sound of the crowd inside.

The stage was draped in metallic streamers. A low, billowing cloud of fog drifted across the floor. Gold and silver lights blinked on and off in the dream-like landscape.

And then a beautiful girl in a beautiful costume leapt out onto the stage and wove her way with pirouettes and jumps through the glittery scenery.

She was covered from head to foot in sequins. Even her toe shoes flashed sparkles of light as she twirled in place and fell into the arms of another dancer dressed as an astronaut.

I stood at the back, unable to take my eyes off of their beautiful dance. Everyone in the audience was so caught up in the grace of their movements that, when they were all finished, a kind of appreciative hush filled the theater, followed by a thundering round of applause.

As I listened to the clapping, I wondered if I could dance here in Galactica, if I could wear a beautiful costume and perform on stage in front of a crowd. No, I didn't even want to think about the possibility.

But, I couldn't resist walking a little closer to the stage after the audience left and touching the silver streamers.

Without thinking about it, I climbed up on the stage in my working clothes from the kitchen. After a quick glance to make sure no one was watching, I began dancing.

At first, I picked out the steps I remembered from the space girl's dance. And then the music started beating in my head and I leaped across the stage, pounding out my frustrations.

First I moved fast, my heart beating in rhythm with the crashing cymbals in my ears. *Why? Why do we have to move?* I asked myself. The music in my head blared.

Then I twirled slowly, as if I was pleading with my imaginary mother and father, begging them to reconsider. I reached out my hands and then curled them around me. *Please don't go,* my dance steps said.

But my invisible parents didn't listen, and I was left alone with only the strains of ghostly violins in my head. Slowly, sadly, I spun to the floor and cried.

I looked up to catch a fleeting glimpse of the space girl dancer, now out of her glittery costume, peeking from behind the curtain. She must have been watching me from the wings.

By the time I arrived back at the hotel I was more determined than ever to stop the move. Somehow, during the food preparation the next day, I had to switch the spices and ruin Abby's chances for the job.

I knew I couldn't count on my friends to help me. They were too busy having fun. I was the only one trying to save the Forever Friends Club.

We spent the early part of the next day getting ready. I kept trying to find an opportunity to switch the spices, but the kitchen was crowded with people and I would have been seen. It was during practice for our own kiddie show that I finally had the chance to slip away.

Tish, Aimee, Krissy, and Linda Jean were setting up for the kids we were to entertain during the banquet. The banquet hall had a huge stage at one end. Ms. Mitchem had informed us earlier in the morning that she expected 100 children and that she hoped we could handle it!

We assured her that we could. But remembering the disaster we'd almost had at the Georgian School, we decided to change our tactics a little and produce one show, rather than divide the kids into groups.

The party at the Georgian School had also taught us that we had to enlist the help of the older kids in the group so that things didn't get out of hand. It was especially difficult when the kids were all different ages and were all interested in different things.

I knew that now was my chance to carry out my plan. All of the Forever Friends had their heads together discussing tactics for the party. I could escape to the kitchen and mix the spices now—but I had to act fast.

"Umm, I need to go back to my room for some rosin," I told them. "When will you be done practicing your clown act on stage, Krissy?"

"I need about another half hour," she told me.

"I'll be back by then," I said. I couldn't believe how easily the lies were slipping off of my tongue. I wished it didn't have to be this way.

"Wait up!" I heard Linda Jean call as I hurried off toward the kitchen, my rosin already tucked securely in my duffle bag.

I slowed down, but kept walking.

"What do you need?" I tried to ask in my most normal voice, but I knew it came out sounding strained.

"You're in quite a hurry," Linda Jean observed.

"Well, I only have a half hour," I told her. "I have to get my rosin and come back in time to practice."

Linda Jean leveled her gaze at me as she kept pace alongside. "I'm your best friend," she said. "You can tell me if you're upset. You can tell me if you're going to do something besides get your rosin."

"Why would you think that?" I snapped, immediately on the defensive. "I wouldn't lie to you," I lied.

"I didn't say that you would," she said. "It's

just that I'm worried about you. You seem more on edge than usual. I just thought you might want to talk about it."

Linda Jean was being so nice, but I didn't want her to be that way. I didn't want to sit down and have a cozy chat. I had a job to do and I was afraid she would try to stop me.

"I don't have anything to talk about!" I said, my voice nervously loud. "See you later."

But she didn't take the hint and leave. She kept walking with me and waiting for me to say something. I didn't need her sympathy—not now.

Finally she spoke again. "I wouldn't have mentioned anything, except that I noticed earlier that your rosin is already in your bag."

That did it. My nerves snapped and I yelled at Linda Jean. "You were snooping in my bag," I shouted. "How dare you go through my private things?"

"I wasn't snooping," she said, calmly ignoring my outburst. "You told me to get your pen earlier, remember?"

I had asked her to hand me a pen out of my bag, but her calm answer only made me angrier. "That still gives you no right to look through my things! How would you like it if

I checked out your purse?"

I had to get away from her. I started to walk faster.

Linda Jean stepped in front of me.

"Please, Joy, listen to me. I'm afraid you're going to do something stupid and I'm just trying to stop you before it's too late. You're headed for the kitchen, aren't you?"

I tried another tactic. "I don't know what you're so surprised about. I told you I was going to do something to wreck Abby's chances for this job."

"So it was you who hid the ingredients!" she said. "It seemed a little too convenient."

"Good idea, huh?" I asked with a smile that I didn't quite feel. "That really got Abby frustrated."

Linda Jean stood silently, her hands on her hips. "I don't know what's a good idea and what's a bad idea," she said, "but I think you've done enough. You're going to get into trouble, Joy."

"Don't you see?" I pleaded. "I can't stop now. I've almost won."

"No, I don't see," Linda Jean said impatiently. "Look, Joy, I don't want you to move, either, but I don't think rearranging a few items in the kitchen is going to change things. It will just make Abby angry."

I closed my eyes against her probing gaze. I didn't want to involve her and I had already said too much. "I have to go," I said, my nerves stretched as far as they could go.

She put her hand out to stop me as I started to walk past her. "Please, think about what I said, Joy. Promise me you won't hide all the ingredients tonight."

"I promise that I won't hide any ingredients," I said. That was true, after all. "I'll just go get changed for my practice."

She stood there and watched me go. Lying to my friend and leaving her there was the hardest thing I had ever done.

As soon as I was out of her sight I detoured to the kitchen. Great, no one was around! Just to be sure that Abby wouldn't show up and catch me, I picked up the phone and called my parents' room. Dad answered.

I asked him where Abby was.

"She's taking a short rest and will be back down to the kitchen in 30 minutes or so."

"Okay, thanks," I said.

"Is everything okay?" he asked. "Is there anything I can do?"

"N-no. I'm fine. It's nothing important. I'll see her when she gets back. We're all meeting later to make the cinnamon buns anyway."

"How's practice going?"

"Fine." *Stop asking questions, Dad,* I wanted to shout. *I only have 30 minutes.* "Well, I'd better get back to my dancing. I wouldn't want to miss a step tomorrow."

"Your mother and I are very proud of you, Joy. I hope that you know that."

I almost choked. I dropped the bottle of cayenne pepper I was holding in my hand. "I do know that." I also knew how very disappointed they were going to be if they found out that I ruined Abby's job.

But that wasn't enough to stop me. All I had to do was conjure up an image of me all alone in Galactica and my friends having fun in Atlanta to make the tightness in my chest reappear.

No, I wouldn't back out now. I was afraid of what my parents would say if they found out, but I was more afraid of moving.

As soon as I hung up, I went over to the cinnamon container and carefully mixed the whole bottle of cayenne pepper into the cinnamon.

Good. You can't tell. And the cinnamon smells stronger than the cayenne. They'll sprinkle the pepper on without even knowing it.

I dropped the cayenne bottle into my bag with my shoes. I took one last look around to make sure I hadn't left any evidence.

The kitchen looked as sparkling clean as it had when I entered.

# Eight

ONCE my deed was done, I went back to practice. Throughout the rest of the afternoon and during dinner, I was careful to avoid Linda Jean's curious looks.

As soon as dinner was over, we all gathered in the kitchen for our final task before Sunday's benefit—making the cinnamon buns. It was actually kind of fun working in a big kitchen with plenty of room for all of us to do our own jobs. At home, we were always running into each other.

"That's it. The last of the flour," Linda Jean said. "Start the dough hook turning."

Aimee watched the giant, stainless steel dough hook twist and turn around in the equally gigantic, stainless steel mixing bowl.

"Wow, I wish we had one of these at home,"

Aimee said with awe.

"And how about that deep fryer?" Abby asked, pointing to the huge vat heating up by the far wall. "We'll be done cooking the cinnamon buns in no time."

"Thanks for letting us see a little more of the park before we had to go to work tonight," Tish added. "This place is great. I don't think you could ever see it all. I'd love to move here if I had a chance!"

Abby glanced at me, but I looked away. She quickly changed the subject. "Did I show you girls how the microwave dough raiser works?" she asked.

"No," we all said.

"Well, take a look at this." As the dough hook turned, she led us to what looked like a huge microwave oven. "All we have to do is throw the buns in here to rise and they'll be done in a few minutes instead of an hour," Abby explained. "That's why you had time to play before work—because the work will go so fast."

I turned away to check on the dough. It was almost done. It was time to add the cinnamon mixture. We always swirled some into the dough and dipped it on top, too.

"Go ahead and add a cup of the cinnamon mix," Abby called, still standing next to the microwave with Linda Jean. "Then let it mix in until it looks like marble."

My hand only shook a little when I dumped the cup upside down and watched disaster swirl its way into the dough.

Abby suddenly switched off the machine. She looked at me strangely.

*Oh no, did she suspect what I was up to?*

But instead of accusing me of anything, she said, "Looks done to me. Can't daydream on this job, Joy." She smiled at me. I felt my guilt sitting on my chest like a solid lump.

"Sorry," I whispered. But my apology had much more meaning than she knew.

"That's okay, honey. No harm done. Now everyone grab a hunk of dough and start shaping buns. As soon as we've shaped enough buns, Linda Jean will run the raising operation and Aimee will fry. Tish, you sprinkle cinnamon at the far end."

I was glad she didn't pick me for the final crime. I probably would have started crying and ruined my whole plan. But even if I had wanted to stop it now, I couldn't have. It was too late.

And then the door opened and Ms. Mitchem walked in. There was another woman with her who looked almost like her twin.

"Working a little late, aren't we?" Ms. Mitchem asked. "Still having those delays?" She was really in nasty form tonight.

"We're right on schedule. If we made the buns too soon, they would be stale by morning. You're out quite late tonight, too," Abby said pleasantly.

"I just brought my sister over to make sure that you weren't changing too much in *her* kitchen."

"Hi. My name is Kelli Mitchem," the young woman said, reaching out to shake hands with Abby. "How's it going?"

"Just fine," Abby smiled, a hint of suspicion in her eyes.

The rest of us also wondered why Kelli Mitchem would be so nice and polite if she thought Abby was taking her job away.

"See, I told you she would move in as if she owned the place," the older Ms. Mitchem spat. She waved her arm in a sweep that took in the bun rolling table, the draining rack with its film of cinnamon dust, and the racks of buns coming out of the microwave. "What a mess!

This kitchen never looked like this when you were in charge, Kelli," she said.

"Princess, I never had to make food for this many people. And I never had to cater breakfast, lunch, and dinner for the same group in one day like Mrs. Marshall is doing."

Princess? We all grinned at each other. Was that her real name or a nickname? It didn't matter. Ms. Mitchem didn't look or act anything like a princess.

"I'm sure you could with practice," she said in a low voice.

"What are you making now?" Kelli Mitchem asked Abby.

"Cinnamon buns for breakfast," Abby answered.

"Mind if I try one?"

"Oh, no! You wouldn't want to do that," I stepped in front of the rack of cooling buns that Tish had just sprinkled cinnamon on. "You'll burn your mouth."

"Oh, I see. They just came out of the fryer. Well, I'll be careful."

"Go ahead and have one, both of you," Abby offered.

"Abby," I hissed as I raced to her side. "You wouldn't want to feed the competition."

"Oh, nonsense. They'll be eating them at the breakfast tomorrow anyway."

"Thank you. They look delicious," Kelli declared. "I wish I could get my dough to rise so evenly. Would you like one, Princess?"

I was beyond giggling at this point. I could see my whole plan going down the doughnut hole as the Mitchems bit into my spicy buns.

Princess Mitchem walked over to stare at the neat rows of finished buns. "No, thank you," she spat. "And you're supposed to be watching your weight, Kelli, dear," she added. "I wouldn't, if I were you."

"Well, you're not me," Kelli said quickly and took a bite of the bun.

I closed my eyes and felt a buzzing across my nose and up into my head. This was it—the end. I'd be discovered. And when there was still time to make new buns. Maybe I wanted to be discovered. I had just opened my mouth to blurt out my confession when Kelli complimented Abby on the buns.

"Mmmmm, delicious," Kelli said. "Quite a tang. Kind of cajun cinnamon, huh?"

She liked it! I couldn't believe she liked it! Cajun cinnamon? What? Were this woman's tastebuds missing?

I sauntered over to the rack and broke a small piece off of a bun while Abby was saying good-bye to our guests. I popped it into my mouth and immediately my eyes began to water.

I ran for the bathroom just as I heard Abby say, "It was very nice meeting you, Kelli, and seeing you again, Princess."

If I hadn't been crying so much, I might have laughed.

Two hours later we were finished. It was 11:00 and everyone was exhausted, including Abby.

"Let's do one last check to make sure we have made everything for tomorrow and all we have to do is heat and serve," she said, taking out her list.

"Cinnamon buns, juice, the fruit we'll have to do in the morning, the scrambled eggs are mixed, spiced, and ready to cook. Anything else?"

We shook our heads.

She went on. "Let's see, for lunch—the flying pizza saucers are baked, the Galactica sparkling punch is made, we'll toss the salad after we clear up breakfast, and how about the Big Dipper fondue for dessert?"

"We've cut up all the pieces of cake and fruit and they are ready to be dipped in the marshmallow creme fondue sauce. All we have to do is heat it at the last minute," Aimee reported.

Abby scanned her list for the dinner menu and read the items off. "Check," she said, when she was finished. "I hope that everything goes according to plan, because there isn't time for slip-ups at this point. It's either fly or crash. And we know that Princess Mitchem is waiting for splash down.

Dad walked in just then. "Anybody need an escort back to the hotel?"

"Hi, John," Abby said. "I guess we've done just about all we can do here. This is the hardest job I've ever had, but it sure is a challenge," she continued, her eyes glowing. "And I sure like seeing you every day after work."

"Yep, all the traveling sure has been hard on the family. But, maybe if things go well, that part of our lives will be behind us. We'll have a chance to get to know each other again."

Dad kissed Mom right there in the big, silver, gleaming kitchen, but all I could see through my tears were the rows and rows of ruined cinnamon buns.

I was the most selfish kid on the face of the

planet. Or any other planet for that matter. How could I wreck their happiness? How could I be so rotten?

Once again, I was just about to come clean and confess when Abby reached out and grabbed a bun. Before I could open my mouth, she took a big bite and started to chew.

Suddenly, she coughed and spit the bun into the sink. "They're ruined," she shouted, her face turning red as she guzzled a glass of water.

"What's wrong?" Dad asked in alarm.

"Someone must have put cayenne pepper in the cinnamon. I bet it was that Ms. Mitchem. Now we'll never be able to make more in time. The menu already says cinnamon buns. The board of directors will be expecting cinnamon buns. Princess Mitchem will be cheering and moving her sister into my job before lunch. Oh John, what am I going to do?"

As we all watched, stunned, my hold-every-one-together mother burst into tears.

Through her sobs, she recounted the disasters since we had arrived. "(Sob) first the forgotten ballet shoes and the complaints, (sob) the hidden ingredients, the delays, the missing utensils. And now this!"

She buried her face in Dad's shoulder. "It will be all right, Abby," he said as he led her out of the room. "You'll think of something. You always do."

"Not this time, John. Oh, I was fooling myself. No one wants me here. Joy hates it and the Mitchems are hovering like vultures. No, after tomorrow, I'll just tell the board of directors to forget it. We'll go back to Atlanta."

"Come on. Let's go back to the room so that you can get some rest."

Her voice was high-pitched and she was losing control. The last words I heard her say as the door was closing were, "There's no place to buy flour at midnight in Galactica."

# *Nine*

AS soon as the door closed behind Abby and John, the Forever Friends exploded in sound.

"I can't believe this is happening!" Krissy said.

"What are we going to do?" Aimee asked.

"Abby feels terrible. She thinks this is the end of this job...," Linda Jean added.

Then Aimee put forth a theory. "You know, I had the feeling that Ms. Mitchem was up to no good. She was always coming in here, snooping around."

"I'll bet she hid the ingredients and switched the spices," Tish said. "She would do anything to get her sister this job."

"Right," continued Aimee. "And that Kelli seemed so nice. It was probably all an act."

"Poor Abby," sighed Krissy. "She wanted this job so badly."

"I didn't realize how much until now," I said in a low voice. Then suddenly I just couldn't keep my secret in any longer.

"I did it," I whispered.

"What?" four voices responded in unison.

I started to cry. Between sobs, I said, "I didn't want Abby to get the job. I hid the stuff. I left my shoes home on purpose. I put the pepper in the cinnamon."

For a second they all stood there just as shocked as when Abby had broken down a few minutes earlier.

"Why?" Tish asked. "This is a great place. Your mom and dad are going to be together. Any kid would love to live in Galactica."

"Not this kid," I sniffed. "But what do you guys care? You'll be happy if I move."

Great, big, wet tears ran down my face and spotted my Abby's Catering apron.

In a flash all my friends were around me, hugging me, crying with me. "Of course we care," Aimee said. "We don't want you to move either. We know how hard it is on you."

"We haven't made it any easier, though," Krissy said. "I guess we've all been caught up in the excitement of this place. I'm sorry for not being a better friend."

"I thought you all were so happy here," I said.

"But we're not that happy," Linda Jean added. "I told you that already. Oh, sure, all this scientific junk is fascinating, but it's not going to be the same without you in Atlanta. We love you."

"And we'll miss you every day," added Tish. "But we'll always be your friends. Isn't that what you told me when I was having such a hard time about moving?"

"Yeah, but you move all the time," I said. "This is my first time."

"You never get used to leaving people and places behind," Tish said. "You just learn to like new places and meet new people. And you're a really outgoing person, Joy. You'll have everyone in Galactica as your friend in no time at all."

"Isn't there anything about this place that you like?" Aimee asked.

I thought back to my visit to the stage the other night. For a moment I had wondered what it would be like to dance the part of the space girl. "A few things," I answered.

"And it's not as if you're losing a job," Krissy said. "You'll still be working for your mom. We're losing both of you," Linda Jean added.

"I didn't think you cared," I said with a final sniff. "I thought you were glad I was going."

"No way," Linda Jean interrupted. "And we won't be able to have nearly as many parties without our favorite dancer and our favorite caterer."

"Maybe that's not such a bad thing," Aimee said. "We talked before about how Party Time was getting too big and how it was taking up all of our time. I think slowing way down is a good idea, especially during the school year."

"I'm for that," Krissy agreed. "It got pretty crazy last year with school and the business. And I know my homework's going to be even worse this year in ninth grade."

"So you're saying that even if we hadn't decided to move, that Party Time would probably have stopped anyway?" I asked.

I had often wondered myself how we were going to keep up our frantic pace.

"I was just looking for the right moment to bring the subject up," Aimee told us. "I'm glad it's out in the open now."

We all sat quietly in the silver and white

kitchen looking at each other with new under-standing.

"But what are we going to do about the cinnamon buns?" I asked at last. "Abby's ready to give up and I can't let her do that. It's my fault and I have to find a way to fix it. Whether she decides to take the job or not, I want to-morrow to be successful. I owe her that."

"Could I talk to you a minute?" Linda Jean asked me. "In private."

"Sure," I replied with much more enthusi-asm than I felt. We left the rest of the group discussing possible ways to salvage the buns. We put our heads together near the refrigera-tors.

"What are you going to do?" she asked, coming right to the point.

I knew what she was getting at. "I think I'd better go talk to Abby and John. It's time I stopped acting like a spoiled kid and started acting like me."

"Do you want me to go with you?"

I shook my head. "Thanks, but no. I have to face this alone."

"I'll be here when you get back," Linda Jean said.

I could feel tears gather in my eyes as I

walked to the elevators. I tried to tell myself that Abby and John loved me, that they wouldn't be mad at me if I was honest about my feelings. But I knew that wasn't true. They would be mad and they had every right to be. I hoped it wasn't too late to fix things.

I knocked softly on the door of my parents' suite, then again more firmly.

John answered the door. His hair was messed up and his eyes looked tired. I slipped in and closed the door behind me.

"Where's Abby?" I asked. "Is she all right?"

John put his finger to his lips. "She's sleeping. She needs her rest."

I decided to plunge right in with my confession. "I have something to tell you and you're not going to like it," I said.

"We'd better sit down," John said, motioning to the couch in the living room area of our suite.

I sat down and clasped and unclasped my hands. My head felt dizzy, and I thought I might faint.

"I know who switched the spices," I began.

"Who?" he almost shouted, then lowered his voice. "When I find out who's responsible for this, I'll..."

"I did it," I said, half hoping he didn't hear me.

"You?" he asked, a dawning look of understanding in his eyes. "You pulled a stunt like this?"

"I'm sorry."

"Sorry isn't good enough, Joy. You have some explaining to do. I can't believe you would deliberately hurt your mother like this."

"I know. It's not like me at all. I guess I just went crazy when I found out we were going to move. I wanted to stop it somehow."

"What about talking to us? Did you ever think of that? We're not monsters, you know. We're your parents!" He got up and paced the small room. "Well?" he demanded.

"You wouldn't listen," I said in a small voice. "All you and Abby kept talking about was how great it would be. You told me I would get used to it. But I know that I won't. And I had to find a way to stop the whole thing!"

He stopped pacing. "So why confess now?"

I thought for a moment about everything that Liza and Linda Jean had said, then I stood to face him. "I guess I realized that I was being selfish. I was only thinking of me and how much I would lose, not how much the family would gain. Liza tried to explain it. Linda Jean tried to help me to see your side, but I wouldn't listen."

John opened his arms and I went into them. Against my hair, he whispered, "That's a very grown-up thing to admit. But this time you also have to realize that it can't be fixed with an apology and a hug."

"I know," I murmured into his chest. He felt warm and safe, and I wanted to stay there until the world fixed itself.

"You have to tell Abby what you did," he said simply.

"Now?" I asked, raising my head in panic.

"No, I think we should let her sleep."

"But what about the cinnamon buns? Talking hasn't changed the mess I made. If only I had more flour and sugar and yeast. I would stay up all night if I had to. I could make a whole new batch. But there's no way!" I sighed.

"There might be a way," John said.

"But Abby said there was no place to buy flour at midnight," I said. "Or cinnamon or sugar or butter...."

"I have an idea about where to get them.

You write down the recipe," he said. "And I'll take care of the ingredients."

Together we went down to the kitchen and I told my friends about my plan to cook all night.

"I'll help," Linda Jean said right away.

"Me, too," Aimee and Krissy said at the same time.

"I don't have anything else to do," Tish joked.

"You're absolutely the best friends in the world," I said. "I'm sorry I caused all this trouble."

"We're sorry that we all got so excited about Galactica that we ignored your feelings," Aimee said. "I think I was hoping that if we didn't talk about it, it would all go away by magic."

"Well, what I did won't go away unless we get busy." I quickly copied down Abby's list of supplies from the master notebook.

"I'll be back in a flash," John said. "But while I'm gone, I want you all to dispose of the damaged goods and get out the bowls and mixers. When I come back, we'll have the biggest bun-making party this place has ever seen. If we're quick, maybe Abby will wake up tomorrow and will think this was all a bad dream."

I couldn't believe my dad and all my friends were going to help me. I worked harder than anyone else to clean up the mess and set out the supplies to start another batch of dough.

By the time Dad arrived with the ingredients, we had put on fresh aprons and were ready to go. John put on Abby's apron and placed a hair net over his short hair. "I don't know much about baking, but I'm a great organizer," he said. "Just tell me what to do and I'll do it."

"Where did you get the flour and spices, John?" Tish asked.

"I took a quick drive to the Pride Supermarket warehouse. They were happy to lend a hand—so long as Party Time agrees to do a free show for the company picnic sometime in the future."

"Wow, it sure is handy to have a dad with a key to the warehouse. You're the best," I said.

He held up a long wooden spoon. "Now tell me what to stir." We mixed, kneaded, fried, and sprinkled. Without Abby, it took us longer to make the buns, but we just kept working steadily, hoping we would be done in time.

The hours blended into one another until we saw the sky begin to lighten. Dad sat down next to me and I laid my head on his shoulder. He brushed my hair off of my forehead with a light touch. "I didn't realize how hard this was on you," he finally said. "Abby and I were so caught up in the excitement of it all that we didn't pay enough attention to your feelings."

"It's just as much my fault," I said. "I didn't tell you my feelings. I kept them to myself because everyone seemed so happy. All of you—even the Forever Friends—kept talking about how great the move was going to be. I felt like I was the only one who didn't want us to move."

"We should have sat down in the beginning and talked it all out," Dad said.

"It wouldn't have helped, I don't think," I explained as I watched my friends wearily take off their aprons and drop them in the laundry hamper. "I couldn't think beyond my own selfish needs."

"It's not selfish to want to be with your friends," John assured me. "And it's not selfish to be afraid of change. It's scary for Abby and me, too."

"Really?" I asked.

He nodded. "I've never had a job where I had to stay in one place all the time and deal with the same people on a daily basis. I'm used to being independent, and now I'll be responsible for more than 200 people."

"And you don't know a lot of them," I mumbled.

"What?"

"Oh, I was just thinking that you don't know many people here either. And Abby doesn't have any friends here. We're all starting over."

"But there's one important thing," John said, putting his arm around me. "We're doing it together."

I grinned. "You know, I think I might like having my dad around every day."

"And every night," he joked, pointing to the clock. "We'd better finish up here and then get ready for Abby and the big day ahead."

I looked around. "It's almost as if nothing ever happened," I said, kind of hoping that John would forget that he had asked me to tell Abby what I did. But I couldn't get out of it that easily!

"Don't forget to have a talk with your

mother at the first opportunity," he said. "And then the three of us will have to discuss your punishment."

"Staying up all night working isn't enough?" I asked.

He raised one eyebrow.

I shook my head slowly. "I guess not. Otherwise all of my friends would have paid the same price as I did and they didn't even do anything.

He nodded.

"I'll talk to her as soon as I can," I told him.

The rest of the girls gathered around us, looking surprisingly awake for having had no sleep at all. It must be all that practice staying up all night at sleepovers.

I glanced around at everyone. "I promise to do everything in my power to help Abby get this job."

# Ten

"WHAT'S going on down here?" Abby asked, walking in on the scene. "Look, everyone, it's all over. There's no point in..."

Then she sniffed. She looked around the kitchen and sniffed again. "Are those fresh cinnamon buns I smell?"

All of us just looked at her and grinned.

"But that's impossible!"

John walked over and put his arm around her. "Nothing's impossible in Galactica. We just sent the Galaxy shuttle out to the all-night grocery store on Mars. Then we had an all-night cook-a-thon!"

"Won't you girls be too tired to work to-day? We have three banquet meals to serve, plus you have to entertain at the party tonight for the kids."

"We'll manage, Abby," I told her.

"I don't know how you did it, but I'm glad you did. I still don't know about this job, though. It seems as if everyone and everything is against me.

"Abby...," I began, but John put his hand on my shoulder.

"There'll be time for talk later," he said. "Breakfast for 200 in one hour."

I never knew my dad was so good in the kitchen. In fact, I never knew my dad much at all, except on weekends. I was really beginning to enjoy having the whole family around. I knew he'd have to start working during the day soon, but even seeing him every evening had to be better than seeing him only two days a week.

Breakfast went off without a hitch. I saw Princess and Kelli Mitchem seated at a back table with the rest of the board of directors. Princess was scowling. Kelli was talking and joking with everyone.

Lunch went just as well. The compliments flooded in. People stood around the buffet table just to thank us for the excellent food. Several times in the middle of the speeches on coastal protection and conservation, the speaker commented on the great meal.

I wanted to talk to Mom in the afternoon, but she insisted that we catch an hour of sleep between lunch and dinner. After that we had to get ready for our show.

I may be slightly biased, but I think we put on the best performance of our lives that evening.

"How are you doing, Joy?" John came up and asked just before I was getting ready to do my dance.

"Okay. I get a little bleary-eyed when I start thinking about Atlanta and losing my Forever Friends, or not getting to see Russell. But I tell myself that it's not the end of the world, that everyone still loves me, and that having my family together is the most important thing."

"I think that I'm going to start coming to you for advice," he said.

I looked up to see if he was laughing, but his expression was serious. "Have you had a chance to talk to Abby yet?"

"I tried a couple of times, but everything has been so busy."

"Don't wait too long," he cautioned.

On stage a few minutes later, I gathered

the 20 kids I had chosen to help me and told them what I was planning. We were going to play follow the leader, and by doing that we would look like a weaving serpent. As I began dipping and swaying, the children concentrated on following my lead.

Out of the corner of my eye, I saw Abby standing at the back table, talking with the board members. She was shaking her head and I became worried.

What if all the work we had done to save the breakfast was too late? What if Abby was so fed up with all my little bad deeds that she was turning down the job just when I was getting used to the idea?

I danced my way down the steps of the stage and wove in and out of the first tables to the delight of the children's parents. But I wasn't interested in entertainment at this point.

I danced between the tables and past where Krissy was standing. She was ready to amaze the onlookers with her magic tricks.

"I need to talk to Abby," I said as I danced by. "Can the clown take over the dance?"

She nodded once, immediately seeing how upset I was.

"Follow me," she called to the line. "Now

we'll show them how to dance!"

Linda Jean changed the tape and the kids began bouncing in time to Kirssy's wild clown dance. The audience was so busy watching their antics that nobody noticed when I made my way to Abby's side.

I arrived just in time to see Ms. Mitchem grin broadly. Abby was saying, "I'm sorry ladies and gentlemen, but I'm not sure this job is right for me or my family. The stress of the last few days has been overwhelming...."

"Abby, may I talk to you?" I asked tentatively.

"I'm in the middle of something," she said.

"Will you excuse us?" I asked the anxious faces.

"Talk her into it, Joy," Kelli said. "We really need Abby's Catering at Galactica."

I smiled at her. "I'll do my best."

"You're not going to change my mind. I just wasn't meant to have this job. Someone just doesn't want me here and if I stayed, things would just get worse."

"Abby, it was me all along," I confessed. "I hid the ingredients. I ruined the buns. I'm the one who wanted you to give up and go home."

She stared at me for a long moment, looking like she didn't believe a word that I was saying. Finally her shoulders slumped. Instead of yelling at me, she said, "Then turning down the job is still the best thing. I didn't realize that you were so unhappy. Oh, honey, you know I would never do anything to hurt you."

I cringed. "I can't say the same for me. But, I'm sorry. I had a long talk with Dad and I know how much this move means to the two of you, I really want you to take this job."

"Are you sure?" she asked.

I gave her my biggest hug and pointed her back to the waiting group. "I'm sure. And Abby, we'll talk later about my punishment. I really think I should have one."

She grinned. "Wait a second! Who's the parent here?" she asked.

Just as we arrived back at the Mitchems' table, the audience erupted into applause. Party Time had just finished its final act, and I hadn't even paid attention. But it didn't seem so important now.

"Have you decided?" Kelli asked. "We all hope that the answer is yes."

"The answer is yes," Abby said smiling. "My very unselfish daughter here talked me into it."

"Not unselfish, exactly," I murmured.

"Speaking of unselfish," Abby said in a voice low enough for only Kelli Mitchem to hear. "Why are you so anxious for me to take this job?"

"Just between you and me, Abby, I never wanted this job," Kelli said. "I'd love to help out, but I don't want the whole responsibility. Being on the board of directors is tough enough. And the two banquets that I put on practically gave me an ulcer. But there's no talking to my sister. She has always been the ambitious one in the family."

"If you'll consider it, I could really use your help. Half of my crew will be living 200 miles away."

"Do you really mean it?" Kelli asked, her enthusiasm lighting up her face. "You can count on me. I'll even be there to help you clean up tonight."

"That's not necessary," Abby started to protest.

"Oh, but I want to. This board of directors stuff is pretty dull. I'd rather be where the action is."

"I'm really glad Joy talked me back into this," Abby said to the group once again. All except Princess Mitchem were smiling. "I'm meeting the best people, and I'm sure working with all of you will be very rewarding."

"Well, we're hoping she can talk her friends into one more little 'yes,' Mr. Mitchem said.

Before I knew it, the park's owner had walked to the microphone and held up his hand for the audience to be quiet. "Wasn't that a great performance?" he called out to the crowd.

A roar of applause shook the banquet hall. "Did you kids like Party Time?" he asked.

There was another thunderous roar.

"Do you think we could get Party Time to come back? Say once a month to entertain at our benefits? What do you say girls? We'll pay all expenses, your salary, and give you lifetime passes to Galactica!"

This time the roar was so loud, it was almost deafening. I couldn't tell which was shaking more, the ground or me.

Linda Jean, Krissy, Tish, and Aimee all ran to hug me and Abby and John.

"It's perfect," Linda Jean said. "We'll get to see Joy once a month...."

"At least," Tish added.

Krissy said, "And we don't have to stop

Party Time entirely...."

"But one party a month is plenty," Aimee remarked.

"And I get to have both of my parents around all the time," I added. "And I'll be living in the most advanced city on the planet."

The space girl from the ballet appeared beside me. "And dance for the Orbit Palace, I hope," she said.

I stood there nodding my head in amazement. No words would come out.

Kelli laughed. "I think Dad is waiting for your answer," she said, tilting her head toward the stage.

"What's it going to be, Forever Friends?" John asked.

"No doubt about it," I said. "The answer is one...two..."

As I counted I looked at my friends one by one. I knew this move wasn't going to be easy. I was still scared of all the change, but I guess it was part of growing up. And I felt as if I had been doing a lot of that in the past 24 hours.

I took one more deep breath and said, "...three!"

Then we all shouted together...

"YES!"

## About the Author

CINDY SAVAGE lives in a big rambling house on a tiny farm in northern California with her husband, Greg, and her four children, Linda, Laura, Brian, and Kevin.

She published her first poem in a local newspaper when she was six years old and soon after got hooked on reading and writing. After college she taught bi-lingual Spanish/English preschool, then took a break to have her own children. Now she stays home with her kids and writes magazine articles and books for children and young adults.

In her spare time, she plays with her family, reads, does needlework, bakes bread, and tends the garden.

Traveling has always been one of her favorite hobbies. As a child she crossed the United States many times with her parents, visiting Canada and Mexico along the way. Now she takes shorter trips to the ocean and the mountains to get recharged. She gets her inspiration to write from the places she visits and the people she meets along the way.